Hit & Run

Sometimes moving on isn't an option.

Three Ghost Stories

F.I. Goldhaber

Hit & Run

Sometimes moving on isn't an option.

Robert Linden just wanted to forget what happened the night before. But some things insist you remember them.

Royal Blood

Blood spilled centuries past stains the present.

To drive his ancestor's voice from his head, James bribes the ghosts of those who killed him.

Crossroads

Sometimes our destination chooses us.

Three women take refuge in a cozy cottage on the side of the road, but the shelter offered does not exist.

F.I. and Joel Goldhaber live, love, and write together in the Pacific Northwest, sharing their home with three cats including the infamous Editor Kitty.

As a reporter, editor, business writer, and marketing communications consultant, F.I. Goldhaber produced news stories, feature articles, essays, editorial columns, and reviews for newspapers, corporations, governments, and non-profits in five states. Now, her poems, short stories, novelettes, essays, and reviews appear in paper, electronic, and audio magazines, ezines, newspapers, calendars, and anthologies. She published five erotica novels and a novella under another name.

In addition to paper, electronic, and audio publications, F.I. shares her words at events in Portland, Seattle, Salem, Keizer and on the radio. She appeared at venues such as Wordstock, Oregon Literary Review, PDX SynesthiA, bookstores, libraries, and community colleges; gives presentations on subjects as diverse as marketing, writing erotica, and building volunteer organizations; and taught Introduction to Indie Publishing at Portland Community College and as a weekend intensive.

Joel Goldhaber creates unique custom website designs and works with clients to help them manage their web presence, serving as on-call webmaster for half a dozen authors and small businesses. He also uses his vast knowledge of genre fiction to produce stunning book covers.

In addition to his design, web development, and computer programming skills, he wrote reviews and articles about game design that *Knights of the Dinner Table* and on-line forums published. He also writes science fiction, fantasy, and horror short stories and designs role playing game systems.

http://goldhaber.net/
http://fantasticworlds.net/

Hit & Run: Three Ghost Stories
Includes:
Hit & Run
Royal Blood
Crossroads

Fantastic Worlds Publishing

ISBN: 978-1-937839-24-6

Copyright © 2014 by F.I. Goldhaber

Fantastic Worlds Publishing
http://fantasticworldspublishing.com
P.O. Box 80766
Portland OR 97280

Table of Contents

Hit & Run

Sometimes moving on isn't an option.

F.I. & Joel Goldhaber

Hit & Run

By F.I. & Joel Goldhaber

A beam of light from a street lamp shot through the living room window. Robert Linden yanked his aching head away from the brightness and fell off his leather sofa. Blinking rapidly, he tried to manufacture enough moisture in his eyes to unstick the contact lenses he had forgotten to remove. A shape in the shadows surrounding him nagged at the edges of his consciousness.

"Who?" His swollen tongue made it difficult to force the word from his mouth.

Squinting through the painful gleam, he focused on a female form. She wore a stained, blue-gray, thigh-length Gortex jacket and cheap knock-off hiking boots, all scuffed and scratched. A multi-colored, tasseled scarf was draped around her neck. Her faded blue jeans were frayed around the hems and had wet splotches from her knees down. Water dripped from her coat and boots, darkening the pale blue Persian carpet covering his polished hardwood floor.

"How did you get in here? What do you want?" The tightness in his throat made the words sound squeaky.

"I'm Alice Jackson." She ran a finger along the bottom edge of the sixty-inch plasma television mounted on the wall. "I never had anything this nice." Reaching above the shelves of media equipment, she caressed the electric blue Chihuly glass. "Pretty."

Robert cringed. "Get your hands off my sculpture before you break it. " He gripped the seat of the sofa to pull himself off the floor, struggling to maintain his balance as he rose to his feet. "Who the hell are you and what the devil are you doing in my apartment? I want you to leave."

She shrugged and her arms dropped back to her sides. "I can't do that."

He extracted his iPhone from the pocket of his chinos and pointed it at her. "Get out, or I'll call the police."

She cocked her head. "That's a good idea. You can tell them how you drank too much at the Elysian, almost hit two cars on the bridge, raced down Admiral Way in the rain at sixty miles an hour, and didn't bother to stop and see what you hit in the crosswalk at Forty-Ninth."

The chill of an ice cube worked its way from the base of Robert's spine to the nape of his neck. "How the hell do you know all that?"

She stepped forward into the beam of light. Blood matted her brown hair to her cheeks, and she stared at him with eyes so dark they almost appeared black. Bruises covered her pale skin. Metal rings pierced her mangled upper lip, the left nostril of her broken nose, and her skinned right eyebrow. What he thought was water flowing down her coat, was blood, pooling onto the carpet. His stomach heaved and he put a hand over his mouth.

Alice smiled, revealing only a few stumps left in her bloody gums. "Because I'm who you hit."

Robert leaned his elbows on the glass of his desktop and massaged his temples. His stomach roiled, and his eyes still felt like sandpaper. He swivelled his leather chair around and opened the top drawer in the credenza behind him, extracting a bottle of aspirin and a vial of eye drops. Swallowing three tablets without water, he tilted his head back, and squeezed artificial tears into his eyes.

When the throbbing subsided enough for him to think, he searched online for any reference to an accident.

Alice Jackson, 23, of West Seattle was

killed early Monday morning by a hit-and-run driver at the intersection of Forty-Ninth and Admiral Way.

Police have asked that witnesses or anyone who might have pertinent information contact Crime Stoppers by phone or email.

A clerk at the Centaur Exchange used bookstore for the past five years, she volunteered at Gatzert Elementary School and helped build a Habitat for Humanity house last year.

She is survived by her mother, Grace Jackson, and a younger sister, Lizzy.

Robert pushed himself back from the laptop screen. Hands trembling, he reached behind his chair for the bottom drawer and extracted a black-labeled bottle of Johnnie Walker from behind the hanging files. He poured three fingers into one of the crystal glasses next to the water carafe on the glass tray at corner of his desk. Replacing the bottle, he used both hands to lift the glass to his lips. The liquid burned his throat, but eliminated the chill and helped him steady his nerves. *You're just imagining things. Too much whiskey, not enough sleep. No way this is real.*

"Of course, it's real." Blood dripped off Alice's coat onto the pale office carpet. "Sylvia and Jim, the owners of the Exchange, are pretty upset. I knew most of the people who shopped there, what kind of books they liked, whether they were readers or collectors. My cats already miss me.

They're moping around the apartment, waiting for me to come home and play with them and pet them." Alice wrapped her arms around her thin waist, her hands almost touching behind her back. She stared at Robert for a minute. "Of course, I won't come home to them, will I?"

"Shut up. You're not here. You're just a figment of my imagination." Robert downed the rest of his whiskey and set the glass back next to the water carafe with a clink.

Gina Smith stood just outside the cracked open door of his office, her knuckles poised inches from the wood, her eyes open wide enough for her eyebrows to disappear under her bangs, staring at the glass he had just emptied.

"Yes, Gina?"

She jerked up her head and looked into his eyes. Her hand gripped the door knob. "Bad time?"

"Of course not." Robert closed the laptop. "Come on in."

Gina approached just close enough to set a folder on the edge of his desk. Alice scooted closer to Gina and looked her up and down. She reached out and caressed the silk of Gina's white blouse, leaving red stains on the sleeve.

"Simone needs another estimate for the Peterson account." Ignoring Alice, Gina nudged the folder slightly closer to Robert.

"She's pretty." Alice turned to him. "I can see why you did the nasty with her in the broom closet."

"That's none of your business!" Robert shouted.

Gina stepped back. "What?"

Robert reached for the folder. "Sorry, Gina. I've been under a lot of pressure, recently. I'll get on this as soon as I can."

"Of course." Gina turned and scurried out of the office, stepping in a pool of Alice's blood, leaving red footprints in her wake.

This time Robert didn't bother with the glass, but took a swig directly from the bottle. He pressed the intercom button on his phone. "Cecilia, I'm taking an early lunch." He didn't wait for her response, just grabbed his jacket and bolted for the elevator.

Robert pushed through the crowd of tourists. Alice trailed behind him, leaving streaks of red blood on the sidewalk and the coats of people brushing by her. No one else seemed to notice.

"My little sister's probably the most upset. Lizzy's only twelve. Mom got married again a few years after my dad died, and the new guy wanted his own kid." Alice played with the long, yarn tassels on the ends of her scarf. "I used to call her every day; take her to the movies on Sunday afternoons; help her with her homework during the week. Of course, she never needed any help with math and science, just English and Spanish, my best subjects."

Another man jostled Alice and walked away with blood staining the Mariners' logo on his sweatshirt.

"Lizzy just cries and cries and cries alone in her room; won't let anyone comfort her. My mom's real worried. Doesn't know what to do."

Robert jammed his hands in his pockets. "Shut up," he said. "You're not here. You're not talking to me. You're a delusion, an image stuck in my brain that it hasn't parsed yet. Obviously no one else can see you, so you're just a figment of my imagination." He hunched his shoulders, and marched as quickly as he could manage down Seneca Street toward the waterfront and Alaskan Way. "And right now I'm just going to forget you."

At Pier 56, Robert pushed open the door to Elliott's Oyster House.

"Ah, Mr. Linden," the host behind the podium said. "Your usual table, sir?"

Robert followed him past the long, mahogany oyster bar to a table in front of the window looking out onto Elliot Bay. Alice slid into the booth across from him, smearing blood and gore onto the upholstery.

Robert rubbed his temples. "Is it necessary for you to ruin the furniture?"

"Was it necessary for you to kill me?"

Sam sat a paperboard coaster in front of Robert. "Usual scotch and soda, Mr. Linden?"

"Skip the soda today, Sam."

"You drink a lot, don't you?" Alice asked.

Robert held the menu in front of his face. Sam returned with his drink and Robert gulped half of it down.

"Anyone joining you today, Sir?"

Robert shook his head.

"Our lunch special is fresh asiago crusted Dover sole. We also have fresh Alaskan king, sockeye, and coho salmon. You can order any of those alder planked, grilled, or Cajun pan seared."

"Wow!" Alice said. "Those *all* sound yummy. Wish I could try some. Of course, my stomach ruptured when your tires drove over me." She pulled the front of her jacket, blood oozing through the zipper, away from her chest and peered inside. "Can't really eat, now. It'd all just run out."

Robert put the back of his hand to his mouth for a moment, then looked up at Sam. "Not now, Sam. Maybe later." He sipped at his scotch.

Sam moved on to the next table and Robert heard him reciting the specials again. His stomach churned. "What exactly do you want from me?"

"I can't want anything, anymore. I'm dead." Alice shrugged. "But, I don't have anything to do, either. Except follow you."

He emptied his glass and Sam appeared to take it. "Another drink?"

Robert nodded. When Sam disappeared, he put his elbows on the table and leaned forward. "Yes, I've been drinking a lot lately. And that's the only reason you're here. You're a hallucination. I'm not even sure I hit anyone last night. I probably just created you out of guilt for driving a little too fast and a little too drunk. You're just something my addled imagination dreamed up. And when I sober up you'll go the way of pink elephants and bugs crawling up the walls."

Alice smiled, revealing the jagged, bloody stumps in her mouth. "Trust me. I'm real." The corners of her mouth turned down. "The students I read to every week at Gatzert looked so sad, so frail this morning when the counselor told them I wouldn't come back. Gatzert never has enough volunteers, I don't know if someone else is going to read to them the rest of the year. They really need the attention. Dustin doesn't have a mother and his father's always pawning him off on relatives. He never knows in the morning where he's going to sleep that night. And Jessica..." Alice sighed. "I think she's been molested. I wasn't sure, so I never told anyone. I should have said something to her teacher so she could get her some help."

Robert glared at Alice. "I could have made all of that up. You sound too good to be true, anyway."

Sam returned and set another glass in front of Robert. "Were you ready to order lunch, Mr. Linden?"

Robert shook his head. After Sam left, Alice coughed so hard one of her remaining teeth flew across the table and splashed into his glass along with drops of her blood. Robert pushed the glass away.

"Can't seem to stop falling apart. Don't know what I'm going to look like if this keeps up." She nudged the glass back in his direction. "Aren't you going to drink that? After all, if I'm just a product of your imagination, there's no tooth or blood in your scotch, so no reason for you to not drink it."

Robert picked up the glass and stared at the bloody clump of flesh and bone at the bottom. He closed his eyes, pressed the cold glass against his lips, and tried to force his hand to tip it toward him. Finally, he slammed the glass on the table, stood up, tossed down a couple of twenties, and stomped his way out of the restaurant. Alice followed.

Just outside the restaurant, the flashing lights of a police motorcycle that had pulled over at the corner of Seneca and Alaskan Way caught Robert's eye. The officer had one foot on the bumper of a late-model beamer, balancing his ticket pad on his knee. Robert spun on his heel and strode north toward University Street.

"You think the police got a good description of your car after the accident?"

"Just shut up."

"I wonder if they've traced the car to you, yet. Can't be that many Cayenne hybrids in West Seattle. Think they have a 'Be on the lookout' notice out for you? I think that's what they call it, at least on television."

"Shut the fuck up."

"Maybe they're waiting for you. At your office. With a warrant."

"SHUT UP." His spittle sprayed her face.

The police officer looked up from the ticket he was writing and stared Robert up and down. Robert turned left onto Pier 57 and walked toward Elliott Bay. As soon as he was out of the cop's line of vision, he leaned against the building and took deep breaths, trying to slow his racing pulse. Alice stood staring at him. He dialed Cecilia's number, holding the phone tight against his ear, trying to hear over the roar of the wind and the traffic on Alaskan Way. "Cecilia is...is there anyone looking for me this afternoon?"

"Just Simone. She wants to know when you'll get her the numbers for the Peterson account."

"Anyone else?"

Cecilia hesitated. "Like who?"

Alice tugged at his sleeve. "You know if the police are there, they'd tell your secretary to try and stall you so they could trace the call. And, they'd tell her not to tell you they're there."

Robert could hear his heart pounding. "Look, Cecilia. I'm not feeling well. I'm gonna head home."

"But, Simone said..."

He cut the connection and walked back to University Street. The cop at Seneca had disappeared.

"You going into hiding? You know you can't use a credit card, right? They can trace it." Alice had to practically run to keep up with him.

He charged uphill to First Avenue, turned left, and ducked into the first porn theater he came to, paying cash for a ticket and praying Alice wouldn't follow.

Sitting in the dark, ignoring the larger-than-life naked bodies on the screen and the old man jerking off in the row in front of him, Robert tried to regroup. Alice sat down next to him. "Couldn't you have picked a real movie theater?" She looked up at the screen. "That's disgusting." She surveyed the theater and the handful of males scattered about. "Good idea to duck in here, but what will you do when they close?"

Robert shook his head. "Don't know," he whispered. "I just need time to clear my head, to sober up so I can figure out what to do."

"Why didn't you do that before you drove home last night?"

"Oh give it a rest. Your routine is getting old."

"Sorry, death is really all I have to think about now." She wrapped her arms around her waist. "Seriously, what are you going to do?"

Robert sighed. He didn't have the resources, or the will, to go on the lam. "I guess I'll call Steve. My lawyer. Turn myself in." He gripped the seat back in front of him and pulled himself up. The worn, vinyl seat next to his was empty.

Outside, the sun had set. Robert wondered how long he'd sat in the darkened theater. He turned up Seneca, heading back to the office, but when he reached the building, he just kept walking. He fingered his iPhone, knowing he should try to catch Steve before he left his office. Tired of walking uphill, he turned right on Ninth. Blocks away, the lights of St. James Cathedral beckoned him.

He climbed the steps, eased the heavy bronze door open just enough so he could slip inside, and waited a few moments for his eyes to adjust to the brighter light within. Then, he skirted the stone baptismal font and entered the immense sanctuary, crossing himself as he approached the massive white altar in the center. The open doors of the confessional caught his eye and he wandered in that direction. A figure, visible through the lattice, waited in the priest's compartment. He entered one of the penitent's booths. Kneeling, he clasped his hands against his forehead.

The screen slid open.

"Bless me Father, for I have sinned. It's been fifteen years since my last confession and I think I may have killed a woman last night."

"What have you done, my son?"

"I drove home, drunk. I felt a bump, didn't realize I'd hit anyone. But I saw a notice in the paper. A young woman. Hit and run."

"What do you intend to do, my son?"

"Call my lawyer. Face the music. But first, I need absolution."

"No."

Robert looked up, startled.

"I'm sure your high-priced attorney will get you off with a mere slap on the wrist. Probably, probation. Maybe a few months in jail." The priest's voice resonated throughout the church. "How will that balance against the death of a woman who had her whole life in front of her? Against the pain you've caused her family, the loss to her community?" The last words emanated in Alice's voice.

Robert slammed the door to the confessional open and tumbled out. Alice emerged from the center compartment, her blood dripping on the polished white marble of the floor.

"This is a house of God." He tried to yell, but his voice squeaked. "I'm trying to make amends. What right do you have to be here?"

She laughed. "What right do *you* have to be here?" She stepped in front of him. "When I died, I expected God and Jesus, angels and light, like my mother and the priests described." Her voice changed, deepening and reverberating off the stone pillars. "But all I got is cold and darkness, just darkness and cold." Her mouth and eyes sank into pits of blackness. "Cold and darkness." Blood ran down her coat in crimson rivulets.

Robert turned and ran down the aisle, slamming the bronze door open, tearing down the steps. Out of the corner of his eye, he saw headlights, and then pain enveloped his body as something slammed into him. The world spun end over end — then stopped suddenly, although his body continued to shudder. Horrible pain shot through his side. He couldn't breathe. With a screech from its tires, the car sped away. He pushed himself up, but he couldn't get his legs to move, couldn't even feel them. His arms lost strength and he landed face first onto the asphalt. He twisted his head to one side. "Help," he whispered weakly. "Please, someone help me."

He heard shouting voices and footsteps. Someone yelled, "Call the police!" Another voice cried out, "Did anyone get the license plate?" From behind him he heard a girl say, "Oh my God, he's bleeding."

The street lights faded. A dark form, shaped somewhat like a woman, pushed through the circle of people. It bent over him, slowly filling his vision. The shouts of the crowd ebbed into murmurs. He tried to turn away, tried to focus on something, anything else. The form blocked all else out and then there was only darkness.

Cold and darkness, just darkness and cold.

Royal Blood

Blood spilled centuries past stains the present

F.I. Goldhaber

Royal Blood

By F.I. Goldhaber

I stood on the Big Island in front of the mound of boulders that the Hawaiians called Hikiau Heiau — the ancient temple at Kealakekua Bay, where Captain James Cook met his death in 1779. Sunlight so bright it hurt my eyes danced across the waves pummeling the shore. The salt breeze dried sweat from my skin.

Along the sidewalk between the temple and the carpark, dark-skinned women hawked their crafts from card tables under red, yellow, and blue canvas gazebos. They peddled shiny green baskets woven from lauhala leaves, coconut shells carved into honu turtles and dolphins, and kapa cloth made from wauke tree bark and painted with red and yellow geometric patterns.

"I thought they stopped making kapa when we introduced them to weaving." Cook's ghost grated in my mind.

I sighed. On previous trips to the islands, I had enjoyed the music of the pounding surf and the songs of native birds. This time the damned ghost drowned out the more pleasant sounds with his constant chatter.

Scanning the merchants, I spotted a miniature Akua Loa hanging from a cord around the neck of the oldest woman there. Lono's pole — a carved human head at the top and a square white tapa crosspiece with feather streamers — rested on her chest above a rather impressive bosom. Figurines of Hawaiian deities carved from ironwood covered her table and a nene goose slept under it with its head beneath its wing. Incongruously, a Zulu mask, its dark wood painted with splashes of red and its eyes surrounded with shell beads, was tied to one of the poles supporting her red gazebo.

I ducked into her shade. "Good morning, Madame. I am James Cook Thomas, descendent of Captain Cook. Are you the temple guardian?"

"Cook died here, cursed. No children, no grandchildren, no descendants." A meter or more of glossy, silver-streaked black hair was piled on top of her head and the scent of Pikaki Lani flowers wafted from her skin. She wore baggy bluejeans, a purple shirt with white flowers, and sneakers with the backs mashed down under her heels.

"At least these people cover themselves, al-

though I still can't believe how many women now think it acceptable to wear trousers." Despite more than a decade of practice, I still couldn't tune out the Captain's incessant chatter.

"On the contrary, Madame, he unknowingly fathered a daughter with a Tahitian woman and she is my ancestor."

"Hmmmph. I suppose she has the audacity to think her ancestor's curse prevented my legitimate heirs from producing children."

The woman cocked her head to one side. "You too Haole; no Tahitian blood."

I shrugged. I'd known my dark blond hair and pale skin would impede my quest. "Cook's daughter married a British sailor. My family has lived in Australia for nine generations, now."

She crossed her arms under her ample breasts. "I'm descended of High Priest Kao who ate Cook's liver."

"What gall. I knew they practiced human sacrifice, but cannibalism? And she's proud of it? How disgusting."

I bowed to the woman. "Then you're the one I seek. I need to spend a night atop the temple, to appease my ancestor's ghost." Or at least get his earbashing voice out of my head.

"Only royal blood can climb on Hikiau Heiau."

"These heathen have no claim to a King's lineage."

"High Priest Kao and King Kalani'opu'u," I pronounced the names carefully, "accepted Captain Cook as the embodiment of Lono, god of agriculture and prosperity. That should qualify me, his descendant, as royalty, at least for one night."

"Oh, that chieftain. With the absurdly long, unpronounceable name. He wore a bunch of feathers and stuff. Nothing royal about him."

My curiosity got the better of me. "May I ask why you have a Zulu secret mask in your gazebo?"

She smiled, teeth white against dark skin. Her pidgin English disappeared and I had to wonder what kind of game she ran on tourists. "The church sent my grandson to South Africa on his mission. I didn't want evil spirits to follow him home, so I flew over there to sever them from him." She touched the mask. "I bought this from an old sorceress for protection."

I hoped it worked better for her than the similar Zulu mask I had used to try and exorcize the Captain, my constant companion of the last eleven years.

"Church. At least someone's attempted to convert these pagans. Can't have done a very good job, though, if they still believe all that sorcery foolishness."

"You're Mormon?" Bloody hell, that would make things more difficult.

She nodded.

"What's a Mormon?"

"But you practice the Hawaiian traditions?"

"Jesus appeared in different ways to different people. The gods Lono, Ku, and Kane brought the Trinity to the Hawaiians."

"What a load of poppycock."

I jammed my fists into the pockets of my Dockers. "Interesting theory. But, we digress. I need to spend tomorrow night, February fourteenth, on the temple."

"The anniversary of your ancestor's demise. But why now?"

"Because tomorrow I will turn fifty-one."

She nodded. "Same age he was when he died here." She closed her eyes and took a deep breath. "What do you wish to do?"

Knowing her religion, I dared not share the specific instructions. "The spirits told me to go alone and tell no one what I did or what I saw." Close enough to the truth for my purposes.

"*What makes you think I have any interest at all in appeasing those murderers?*"

She chewed on her lip. "Who gave you the spirits' instructions?"

"An Aboriginal Dreamkeeper followed the songlines to find this path for me." In desperation, after spending years in therapy, I'd paid half a dozen spiritual hacks for charms and spells to chase the voice from my mind. Nothing had worked. If this expedition didn't silence him, I feared I would go mad or resort to suicide to get relief.

"The ones you Australians call Aborigines ... Eingana, Gnowee, Walo brought the trinity to some of them. The Djanggawul siblings represented it for others." She touched the Akua Loa on her neck. "You will not take another onto the temple?"

I had to wonder how she knew so much about other primitive religions, but didn't want to get distracted again. I shook my head, crossing my fingers inside my pockets. Technically. I wouldn't bring another *living* being. I hoped she wouldn't interrogate me about the method the Dreamkeeper had prescribed: arrive at dark, serve beer to the ghosts who would assemble at the temple altar before the moon rose, acknowledge my ancestor's transgressions, and beg forgiveness. The Dreamkeeper couldn't tell me *why* appeasing the Hawaiian ghosts would quiet my ancestor's voice. But, she did warn me that any deviation would doom me to carry him with me for the rest of my life.

"I will grant your request." She tore a receipt off the pad resting on top of a carved ironwood box, scribbled a note on the back, and handed it to me. "If a security guard questions you, show him this."

"*Why do they need guards to protect a pile of rocks?*"

I arrived at the empty carpark at sunset the next day. I had created a sling to carry the heavy keg and hoisted it onto my shoulders using the straps. Heading toward the temple, I carried my torch, loaded with fresh batteries, in one hand and a sack with the kegger tap and a hundred plastic cups in the other.

The carved stone plaque commemorating my garrulous ancestor's ignoble death stared at me from a cement obelisk.

A rope hung across the temple stairs with a sign warning Haole to stay away. When I tried to step over it, several opeapea bats, swooping about after insects, threw me off balance. Before I could regain my equilibrium, I thought I felt a shove and fell to my knees. The sharp pain in my right knee where it hit the edge of the step caused me to cry out. I heard a cackle of laughter above the pounding surf. The beer sloshed, but I gripped the straps and managed to keep the keg on my back.

I heard boot steps approaching from the opposite side of the temple. Struggling to my feet, I examined the torn knee of my pants leg and the stains of red clay from the mud coating the steps. Sticking a finger inside the rip, I brought it back out covered with glistening blood.

A torch beam caught me in the eyes and I put an arm in front of my face to block the sudden brightness. Then I saw the light reflecting off a small revolver. "I have the temple guardian's permission."

"Haole aren't allowed on the temple and no one is permitted in the park after dusk."

I pointed my at my chest. "She gave me a note. May I get it from my pocket?"

"*What makes you think this behemoth will believe she wrote that? He'll probably just shoot you.*" Apparently the Captain could see better in the dark than I since, with the torchlight shining in my eyes, the only thing I could describe about the man confronting me was his deep voice.

"Go ahead."

I extracted the slip of paper from my shirt pocket and held it out at arm's length. I heard the snick of the safety on the revolver and it disappeared from view. I let go the breath I'd been holding. A hand took the paper and he moved the light so it shone on the note.

"Hmph." He handed it back. "Never seen her do anything like this before. I guess I have to let you continue — she's the boss. Try not to make so much noise." The torch flicked off and I heard him walk away.

"If you weren't such a milksop, he wouldn't even have heard you."

I took a hesitant step forward. My knee hurt like hell. But according to the Dreamkeeper, her rituals would only work on my fifty-first birthday. Tonight offered the one opportunity in my lifetime to silence the interminable voice.

Cook first whispered in my ear eleven years ago on the twenty-fifth of August. I later realized that was the two-hundredth anniversary of the day he first sailed from Plymouth, England aboard the *Endeavor*.

In the beginning, he only commented occasionally, usually when I got upset or excited. Soon he voiced opinions on the minutiae of my daily life, knocking everything from my choice of career to my dinner selections. Now he invaded my dreams, obstructed my concentration, and inhibited my libido.

If I didn't silence him, he would drive me insane.

I dragged my throbbing knee up the dozen or so steps, and swept the light of my torch across the wide expanse. I finally spotted the raised stone altar and the remains of a raised wooden platform near the opposite side, almost 70 meters away. Hairs rose on the back of my neck and sweat beaded up on my forehead.

"I can't believe you brought me back here. Do you know what those cowards did to me after they stabbed me in the back?"

My spine felt as if someone was running ice cubes up and down it. I swallowed and brought the light down to my feet so I could find my way without stumbling. The Hawaiians built their massive temples without mortar, and the stones still held together centuries later. But the thirty-six kilos on my back and the piercing pain in my knee made keeping my balance on the rough surface difficult.

A couple dozen meters from my goal, I felt something jerk my left ankle off the rock it balanced on, dropping me down onto my arse. Wrenching pain shot through my leg, and I bit my lip to contain the scream — as much to deter the Captain from hurling invectives at me as to avoid angering the ghosts. Since I hadn't heard anything snap, I could hope I had only strained the joint. When I tried to regain my feet, though, I couldn't find the leverage. I shone the torch at my wristwatch — less than an hour before my window of opportunity closed. My ankle throbbed and I wanted to just give up, to curl up in a ball, and wait until the security guard returned. I wondered if he was Mormon also, or if he'd take the keg in exchange for helping me off this heap of rocks.

"Ha. I knew you couldn't go through with it. You're such a mollycoddle."

I needed to take my life back from that voice. I leaned rearward, resting the keg on the stones, and slipped the straps off my shoulders. Twisting at the waist until I faced it, I pressed my palms against the smooth metal and pushed myself to my feet.

"You're wasting your time, you know. Despite what that she-devil you call Dreamkeeper said, you cannot force me to move on."

Wincing with each step, I lifted the straps, swung the keg a meter or so in front of me. Then I limped across the stones to it and repeated the procedure. I could feel my ankle swelling to twice its normal size and I worried about permanent damage to my knee.

"You really don't think this will work, do you? Just because some old native harpy who claimed to commune with spirits came up with this doltish idea? At any rate, why would you believe I have any interest in moving on?" His voice rasped against my brain. *"You're the first*

male to survive among my progeny. You sit in an office all day pushing buttons instead of doing something useful like I did. If you want me to cease this haunting, take on responsibility worthy of your name."

Years ago, I had given up trying to explain the importance of my job at the Australian Nuclear Science and Technology Organisation. The subject of computer technology had proved impossible for an eighteenth-century explorer to comprehend.

When I finally reached the stone altar, only the stars lit the sky. With no light pollution, I got a reminder of why we call our galaxy the Milky Way. I wondered who would traverse the reaches of the solar system, and whether they would be as much of an arrogant prig as the explorer who haunted me. I leaned against the altar to take some of the weight off my injured legs, pulled the sling straps up, hand over hand, to my chest, and eased the keg onto one of the protruding stones near the altar's corner. Although I looked for dark spots with the torch, two centuries of rain had washed away the blood stains.

A cold chill climbed up my legs and I shuddered. I heard drums and smelled burning kukui nut torches. I felt rather than saw a procession march past. On the one hand I wanted them to stop, to listen, to help me. On the other hand I longed to turn tail and run.

The smell of roasted pig, or perhaps scorched

human flesh, drifted from the empty altar. The latter thought forced me to breathe through my mouth to avoid gagging. Would the ghosts relish the opportunity to sacrifice a live human after centuries of spectral rituals?

"I don't know what you hope to accomplish here. These chaps didn't hesitate to kill me when they were alive. What exactly do you expect from them now that they're dead?"

I grabbed the tap. With the torch in one hand and the tap in the other, trying to get it properly seated on the keg was a bit awkward. But when I pushed down, the seal popped and a spray of foam spewed out. I twisted the tap into place, grateful when the ghostly odors wafted away, replaced by the real-life aroma of hops.

I filled cups with the amber fluid and set them on stones near the keg — three to a stone, as instructed. When I ran out of space that I could reach, I hobbled to and from the further stones, careful not to spill anything. I built a wall of plastic cups along the side of the altar, emptying the keg before the crescent sliver of the waning moon rose. I breathed a sigh of relief — I had completed the required ritual by the deadline. Still, nothing happened.

"Hah! How much have you spent on shysters and gypsies over the past decade? If you'd give as much attention to improving yourself and doing something useful, I might have left long ago."

I thought about the Captain's last visit to Hawaii. The native population had welcomed him and offered to share the bounty of the islands with his crew. In exchange, the Europeans abused the natives' hospitality and brought scorn, death, and disease. I cleared my throat. The Dreamkeeper had given me no guidance on the wording of my apology, only told me I couldn't read anything, that I had to speak from the heart. I thought of all the times I'd scorned Aborigines in my native land or made jokes at their expense. I bowed my head.

"I am James Cook Thomas, descendant of Captain James Cook. I come to atone with a small gesture for the atrocities visited upon you by my ancestor and his kind."

"How dare you speak for me? I brought civilization to these primitives and they repaid me shamefully."

"I would like to make peace with you. If you will help me convince my ancestor, Captain Cook, to move on to the next world, I promise to respect all the world's cultures and teach others to do the same." I took a deep breath. "I have no desire to question or interfere with your decision to stay in this place. But I hope you will accept my gift and free me from the one you welcomed as Lono." Whether he wants to go or not.

"We were never foolish enough to believe your ancestor was Lono." The sonorous voice echoed off the stones of the altar. "We welcomed him because he came during Lono's festival, when we celebrate peace with all. He crew interpreted our goodwill with typical European megalomania. Of course, Cook wasn't that stupid. He just took advantage of our hospitality."

"I never said I thought they deified me. And I'm not a megalomaniac. Where do these savages learn words like that anyway?"

"The Haole abused our welcome during Lono's festival. They returned after the makahiki, and its prohibitions, ended. They tried to take hostages. What did they expect us to do in return? We worship Ku, the war god."

"What can I do to atone for my ancestor's misdeeds?"

Laughter sent chills climbing up my legs again. "You cannot atone for him. He must make amends himself."

I slid down the stone and landed on my sore arse. I may as well find a cliff to jump off, now. I had no hope of getting the Captain to apologize to anyone — especially not if it meant vacating my mind.

I heard shouting, drums, musket shots, and a long, loud wail. Cold chills turned into heat that brought sweat to my forehead and dampened my shirt. I struggled to my feet. The burning smells returned. Three by three the cups of amber fluid vanished. Hints of voices, laughter, even a belch or two drifted around me.

I had saved the hundredth cup for myself. When the last three glasses disappeared from the altar, I lifted it from the top of the keg, raised it to the invisible assembly, and let the warm yeasty flavour slide down my throat. Perhaps it would help anesthetize the pain so I could work my way back across the temple to my car.

At least the keg would weigh considerably less. Given the religious affiliation of the temple guardian, I dared not leave it behind and send someone for it in the morning. Besides, I had promised the ghosts I would practice more respect for their culture. That would include reverence for their holy places.

The smell of salt spray permeated the air, and light tinged the eastern sky. I could hear the ocean pounding on the rocks and a pueo owl hooting in the distance. I listened for Cook's voice, but no words came. No complaints about the quality of American beer or admonitions about my choice of holiday location. I wondered what plans the warrior ghosts had for the Captain. Then I realized I just didn't care. In many ways, he had sealed his own fate with typical British arrogance. If he had left me alone, I wouldn't have dragged him across the Pacific to hand him over to the ghosts of his killers.

I had finally silenced the voice that had haunted me since I turned forty. "Happy birthday to me," I whispered. I slung the empty keg onto my back and started the long, limping journey back across the temple, hoping never to hear a word from the good Captain again.

Crossroads

Sometimes our destination chooses us

F.I. Goldhaber

Crossroads

By F.I. Goldhaber

Agnes glanced at her watch. "We'd better hit the road, ladies, it's going to get dark soon." Susan gathered their empty cups and carried them to the dish tub at the end of the counter, while Lydia rummaged through the pockets of her white Gore-Tex jacket looking for keys.

"Brrr," Agnes said as the three left the warmth of the Keizer, Oregon, coffee shop for the colder-than-usual January air. "Thank goodness this horrid weather didn't keep everyone away from the rally."

Lydia used her remote to unlock the silver Honda sedan. "Won't matter. Even with hundreds at the rally, I bet we don't get much press.

We could have had ten thousand folks crowding the Capitol steps and that pipeline'd still get built. California wants LNG, and no one here has the clout to fight the kind of money the gas company's willing to throw at legislators to get a natural gas line built."

Susan walked around to the front passenger side. "Then why did we freeze our rear ends off at the rally all afternoon?"

Agnes climbed in the back seat. "Because we care." She hoped Lydia wouldn't rant about the futility of their efforts all the way back to Portland. Ten years older, Lydia was the defacto group leader. She had persuaded Agnes and Susan to drive down to the rally in Salem.

Lydia pulled out of the parking lot onto the four-lane road bisecting the bustling commercial district.

Susan extracted the map from the side-pocket in the door and unfolded it. "I'm glad you suggested stopping for mochas, Agnes. At least we got a chance to thaw out a bit. We'll have to remember that place next time we come down here." She fumbled in her purse for her readers, settled them on her pudgy nose, and dragged her finger across the paper. "Oh, dear." She looked up at the road then back down at the map. "We should have stayed to the right when Lockhaven split off back there."

Lydia sighed. "I'll take the next right and we should see signs directing us back to the freeway."

By the time Agnes saw a right turn that seemed more substantial than a subdivision side street, the box stores interspersed with smaller shops had given way first to residential areas and then farmland. Lydia took the turn.

Agnes looked out her window at the frozen stubble of hay fields on either side of the two-lane asphalt road, empty of other traffic. "This doesn't look like it goes anywhere civilized, Lydia."

A mournful train whistle called to the flocks of geese overhead, honking as they flew south in the overcast sky.

"I think you're right. I'm turning around." Lydia stepped on the brakes and pulled toward the small bit of shoulder. Instead, the car hit black ice, spun a quarter of the way around, and skidded broadside toward the train tracks crossing the road. The passenger side tires thudded over the closer rail, and Agnes stared wide-eyed at the light of the freight train bearing down on them. The whistle shrieked over and over again. Lydia gunned the engine, but the wheels just spun on the icy railroad ties.

Agnes pushed herself up onto her hands and knees, the field stubble shredding her pantyhose and cutting into her palms. The train had stopped, the freight cars on the tracks blocking the road. She could see the engine hundreds of yards in one direction, the caboose even further away in the other. The impact must have thrown her clear, although she didn't understand why her seat belt had not kept her in the car. Shakily she got to her feet and brushed the dirt from her brown leather coat. Stumbling over to Lydia, she was relieved to see her friend seemed relatively unscathed. Lydia sat cross-legged on the cold ground, her head in her hands. She only had some small cuts and bruises and smudges of dirt on her jacket. Her steel-grey hair, normally held in place with dozens of bobby pins, spilled over her face. With Agnes' help, she pulled herself to her feet.

They found Susan sprawled on the ground nearby. Agnes needed Lydia's strength to help Susan to her feet. She seemed to have taken the brunt of the collision, with scratches all over the right side of her face, her dyed red hair matted and tangled, and the sleeve of her blue wool coat torn off. Agnes glanced around but did not see a single handbag that might hold a cellphone they could use to call for help. Lydia patted her jacket pockets, and shrugged.

What's become of the car? How could the impact have thrown all three of us clear? Why has no one come back from the train's engine to help us?

Susan pointed to a small brown house with white trim on the other side of the road. "We need to go there to wait."

Agnes wondered how she had not noticed

it before. With Susan's arms draped over her and Lydia's shoulders, the three women limped across the field to the road. Only Lydia had worn sensible walking shoes. Agnes and Susan, hoping that television cameras would cover the rally, had worn heels that sank into the mulching hay waste and made them all stumble.

Smoke drifted from the chimney of the cottage and Agnes hoped that meant someone was at home. By the time they reached the front door, she almost could not support Susan's weight. The door opened just as she wondered if she could take another step.

The man standing in the doorway had black hair streaked with gray that grazed his shoulders. He wore a gray cardigan over a white shirt and black slacks. "Come on in, you're welcome here. I've been waiting for you."

Before Agnes had a chance to protest, he gently scooped up Susan and carried her sideways through the door. Lydia followed.

"Wait!" Agnes stopped at the doorway, unwilling to enter. "What are you doing with Susan? She needs help. The train hit our car, but I don't know where it is." Agnes realized that made no sense; she could see the damn train. She looked inside the cottage. A red sofa and three leather armchairs faced a brick fireplace. Flames danced around a thick pine log, but the room seemed no warmer than outside. Agnes realized that despite the frigid temperature, she did not feel cold. *Must be shock.*

The stranger laid Susan on the sofa and covered her with a red and black afghan. He gestured at the armchairs. "Please, make yourselves comfortable."

Agnes braced herself against the door jamb, unwilling to enter the cottage and become vulnerable to the stranger. But she could not stop her feet from crossing the threshold. She found herself easing onto the chair's cushions, grateful that her injuries didn't hurt. The man left the room and returned moments later with a tray which he sat on the small oak table between Agnes' chair and Lydia's. It held a bright blue ceramic teapot, two white china cups on saucers, a pitcher of milk, a small glass dish full of lemon wedges, a sugar bowl, and a plate of macaroons.

Agnes stared at the refreshments incredulously and shook her head. The man acted as if he expected them, having prepared all the accouterments for tea in advance. But he only brought two cups. And they needed medical attention not tea. Lydia filled one of the cups, set a macaroon on the saucer, and balanced it on the oak arm of her chair.

Agnes dragged her eyes from the tray. "Could we possibly use your phone to call an ambulance? Susan needs to get to the hospital as soon as possible. We," she swept one arm toward Lydia, "probably should get checked over as well."

The man lowered himself into the third arm-

chair, crossed one long leg over the other, and shook his head. "Sorry, don't have a land line and cell phones won't work out here."

"Do you have a car? Could you drive us into town?"

Susan had not moved since the man put her on the sofa. Agnes noticed that the scratches on her face dripped blood that disappeared against the red leather. "She's bleeding."

"So sorry. I'm afraid you'll just have to wait."

"Why? How long? She's not doing very well." Agnes wanted to get up and check on Susan, but she found herself too tired to rise to her feet. Lydia nibbled on the cookie, and the incongruity of Lydia sipping tea while Susan's face dripped blood onto a stranger's sofa made Agnes dizzy.

Susan flung the afghan aside, sat up, and put her feet on the floor.

"You're okay?!" Agnes wanted to jump up and embrace Susan, but could not muster the energy.

"I have to go." Susan placed one hand on either side of her hips, flat against the leather.

"Yes, dear, I know." The stranger reached over and patted Susan's hand as she pushed herself up. "I'm sorry."

"Susan, wait, where are you going?" Agnes stared as Susan walked to the door, pulled it open, and ran outside. The door swung slowly back, to close with a click.

"You haven't even tried the tea." The stranger stood up and poured steaming amber liquid into the second china cup. "Lemon or milk?"

Agnes sniffed but could not detect any fragrance from the cup. Without knowing what type of tea, how could she answer his question? "I don't want any tea, thanks." She turned to Lydia. "Any idea what's with Susan? Why'd she run off like that?"

The stranger offered the pot to Lydia who held out her cup for him to refill. After a few moments of silence he said, "I'm afraid she didn't survive the collision."

Lydia nodded and sipped her tea as if he had just commented on the weather. Agnes stared at him, gripping the wooden arms of the chair tighter and tighter until her knuckles turned white. She released the chair when she realized she could not feel the tension in her braced muscles. She stared at her hands, trying to remember what had happened when the train hit the car. She put a palm on either side of the still-steaming teapot. It should have burned. It did not. Grabbing the fork from the dish of lemons, she jabbed it into her thumb. Nothing.

"What's happening?" She looked up at the stranger, hoping for reassurance, but realizing she couldn't expect any.

He sighed. "Things used to be much simpler. Even with all the new technology you people came up with to prevent death, we still had a good handle on various situations. But, now they have these newfangled electronic thingamajigies in every plane, train, and shopping mall. We started making too many mistakes, escorting folks over only to have someone jolt them back to life." He picked up the full cup and handed it to her.

Agnes took it without protest and sipped even though she knew she would taste nothing. She found some comfort in the ritual, enough to allow her to continue listening to his words without flinging herself out the door into the frigid field to look for Susan.

"We created waiting rooms for folks we weren't sure would die." He swept a hand across the room. "We try to make them cozy and comfortable."

"Nice," Lydia said.

Agnes wanted to weep.

"I can only assure you that everyone is doing their best to keep you two alive until you get to the hospital."

Agnes shook her head. "How bad? I mean, I don't want to spend months in the hospital only to end up an invalid."

"Sorry," he said. "I'm only here to offer you a place to wait until we know one way or the other."

"We have no choice?" Agnes set the teacup back on the tray. Since she had retired, she spent every Tuesday afternoon at the nursing home down the street, reading to patients confined to wheelchairs or their beds. She couldn't, she wouldn't ...

"I'm afraid there's nothing you can do at this point. If you left your family instructions on how to handle such an emergency ..." He shrugged. "Unfortunately, not all families honor those documents. I've had to wait with too many folks who got dragged back against their wishes."

Agnes slumped in her chair, her chin on her chest. She had prepared a living will, but never gotten around to having it notarized. It still sat on her desk at home with other papers that needed her attention.

Lydia startled Agnes out of her self-recriminating thoughts by setting the teacup down on the tray, standing, and walking out through the door. Agnes needed to weep for her two best friends' passing but no tears would come. "She didn't even say goodbye."

"Some do, some don't. Everyone reacts differently." He stacked the empty teacups and carried the tray away. When he returned, he said, "Susan took the worst of it, of course. The train hit her side of the car. We wouldn't have brought her here at all, but since we had to pick up you two ..." He returned to his seat and crossed his legs again. "Because Lydia was much older than you, even though her injuries were not as severe ..." He drew his eyebrows together and frowned.

Agnes couldn't accept what the man said about Lydia's age. Although they met when Lydia returned to school at twenty-nine, her younger friends quickly forgot about the age difference. Even now, Lydia set the pace and Agnes and Susan sometimes had trouble keeping up. Agnes sobbed, a tearless, heart-wrenching wail. She, Lydia, and Susan had been best buddies since they all attended Oregon State together thirty years ago. Her suggestion to stop for coffee in Keizer had cost Agnes her two closest friends and she might not survive either. Worse, she might end up in a wheelchair, or a nursing home.

"Can I find out what's going on, at least?"

He shook his head. "Sorry, all you can do is wait."

Both Susan and Lydia were dead. If she survived the train wreck, Agnes knew her body had to be mangled beyond what she would willingly accept.

"Time to go." She gripped the arms of her chair and tried to push herself to a standing position so she could follow Susan and Lydia out the front door. She could not move. Closing her eyes, she visualized herself walking out the door and pushed as hard as she could against the arms of the chair. Fifteen steps, twenty, she held out her hand groping for the doorknob, but could not find it. Thirty steps. She imagined the cold biting her skin as she left the cottage's warmth. Forty steps. She opened her eyes. She had not moved.

The stranger shook his head. "Would you like some more tea. It looks like you'll be here for a bit."

Agnes groaned in frustration. She had to find a way to break free. She could move her arms, her head, her shoulders. But nothing below the chest would work. "Oh, my god." Agnes wanted to scream. "I'm paralyzed from the waist down, aren't I?"

The stranger moved to the chair Lydia had vacated. "You can't move from your seat because you're in limbo, neither alive nor dead." He patted her hand. "Nothing here correlates directly to what has happened to your body. This is all an illusion." He made a karate chop motion and sank his hand through the arm of his chair.

"I don't want to go back, I don't want to go back, I don't want to go back." Agnes repeated the mantra as if that would release her from whatever might try to drag her there. "Will I remember this if I survive?"

The stranger slowly shook his head.

Agnes pushed her hips forward in an attempt to slide down onto her knees. She stayed in her chair.

No, damn it. She refused to end up incontinent and immobile like patients in the nursing home. Determined to crawl out the door if necessary, she leaned forward in her chair. Eventually gravity would take over and she could pull herself across the floor with her arms. Her head touched her knees. She pushed them apart so she could fall through them to the floor.

The stranger gently lifted Agnes' shoulders

until they touched the back of her chair. When she tried to lean forward again, only her head tilted until her chin rested on her chest.

No, no, no, no. She pinched her nostrils closed between her thumb and index finger and clamped her palm over her mouth. Only then she realized she was not breathing.

"Please ... can't I just move on with my friends?"

He shook his head. "Sorry, all you can do here is wait."

"I've got a pulse." The unidentified female voice entered Agnes' consciousness. Pain raced like wildfire through her body then settled in her chest. The absence of torment in her limbs, given the crushing agony surrounding her heart, terrified her.

Are Susan and Lydia okay? Her lips would not move. She could not swallow. Something blocked her throat, but when she tried to fill her lungs, she realized air was pushing into them. Pain sent her reeling back toward unconsciousness. *What happened? How long was I out?* She remembered the light of the train racing towards the car and nothing more.

Noises and voices bombarded her from every direction. She could not make sense of most of them. Her eyes would not open. Finally, she recognized the sound of slamming car doors and the piercing wail of a siren enveloped her. A male voice spoke behind her. "ETA, 15 minutes. Defibrillated twice. Achieved NSR, rate 90. Intubated, on hundred percent. IV saline. Still unresponsive. MAST pants in place to try to control bleeding from crushed pelvis and leg fractures. Short C-collar to stabilize neck."

His words sent a cold chill through her. She had died. They had brought her back to life and used extreme measures to keep her from bleeding out. Now they thought she had a broken neck. *Stop, please. I don't want to do this. Please, stop.*

"No apparent movement in upper or lower extremities. Orders?"

Agnes heard the response through the static of the radio. "You bringing in one victim or three?"

"Only one."

Oh, my god. Agnes wanted to wail. She could feel tears spilling from her eyes, but could not reach up to wipe them away. *Lydia? Susan?* She wanted to rip the tube from her throat, the IV from her arm, but she could not move. *Please, oh please, let me die, too.* Agnes tried to hold her breath, but something forced air in and out of her lungs. Panic made her heart race. *Calm, I've got to stay calm.* She couldn't control the pace of her breathing, so she tried to evoke the place she imagined when she meditated every morning. Peaceful and quiet, away from the screeching siren. Floating above the lake, among the soft clouds. From serenity, Agnes tried to convince her heart to stop beating. Blackness beckoned. She welcomed its embrace.

In the distance she barely heard, "Oh, shit, I'm losing her again."

Agnes pushed herself out of the chair, walked outside, and slammed the door behind her.

Acknowledgements

Many thanks to all those I have learned from through the years, especially the Wordos professional writers workshop and Larry Brooks. Thanks also to those who have freely shared their knowledge online, notably Dean Wesley Smith and Kristine Kathryn Rusch. Those who inspired me to pursue writing from an early age include Ruth Wright, my fifth and sixth grade teacher at Randolph Elementary School in Huntsville, Alabama; Nancy Travis, my freshman English teacher at Clear Creek High School in Texas; and most prominently my parents, Jerry and Bev Goldhaber. Very special thanks to my editor, Laurie Lawhon of Fine Tune Your Words, and my beloved husband Joel Goldhaber.